Dead Man: Janus City Stories
Episode 1-13

Dead Man

Janus City Chronicles, Volume 1

Lon E. Varnadore

Published by Lon E. Varnadore, 2022.

This is a work of fiction. Similarities to real people, places, or events are entirely coincidental.

DEAD MAN

First edition. February 20, 2022.

Copyright © 2022 Lon E. Varnadore.

ISBN: 979-8201140120

Written by Lon E. Varnadore.

Also by Lon E. Varnadore

A 4Pollack Series
Mostly Human

Janus City Chronicles
Dead Man

Known World Series
Crimson Planet

Starlight Saga
Chain of Starlight

Dedicated to my grandfather

And a special thanks to the cover designer: Oli Price at
www.bonobobookcovers.com

Welcome to Janus City

My name is John. John Gallic. I'm a fixer for the citizens of Janus City. I don't have a home, no cards to advertise or an office to come to for help. Citizens that need my help can find me thanks to the Powers That Be, and I fix their problem. It's what I've done for the past three months. Before that, well, that's a different story.

If someone makes a contract with me, writes the full contract out on vellum, uses the right hexes, and underlines their name in blood as contractor, I'm bound to help them. All thanks to the Powers That Be. Whatever is on the contract, I gotta do. One time, there was an old woman who wanted me to move her from one apartment to another . . . across the hallway. She gave me a homemade pizza and a six-pack of beer after, so I was good with it, especially since she allotted two days and I finished in one.

Why can't they all be like that? I thought to myself as I chased a phazen demon, a low-level grunt of Hell. It had taken over the body of Clarence Goins moments after death and run off. His widow wanted him back. Thought it was going to be easy, then it shrugged off the three silver slugs I fired into the torso. It didn't even wait a heartbeat to bolt. Wasn't expecting that.

I chased it into an industrial park, complete with a construction droid. Lucky for me, we were in an area on the other side of the Barrier, far from Nightside. Demons and their ilk were more powerful closer to the giant wall between the two sides of Janus City. And though I was in Dayside, it did still get dark.

I only had until dawn to catch the damn thing, under the terms of the contract. I rounded the corner I had seen the phazen demon disappear around and was met with a cackling laugh and a trash bin shoved toward me. It caught me in the shoulder, and if I had been mortal, my arm would have been torn off.

Instead, I grunted in pain when the trash bin slammed into me and came to a sudden stop. It's hard to kill a Dead Man. The phazen demon let out a little squeal and, seeing that I wasn't as distracted, rushed me.

My gun was useless, so I drew the one other weapon I had on hand. A silver dagger. As Clarence, his chalky face twisted in a rictus of a smirk, threw a punch at me, I ducked low and stabbed him in the side.

The demon didn't like that. A stain of black ichor oozed from the hole in its side as it screeched and leapt away from me. The ichor stained my blade too, would corrupt the silver if I didn't clean it off later. I'd need to get that crap off soon and hated demons mostly for that reason. Well, that and because they liked to play with the people of this city.

And they hated my kind—those recently returned to life. Dead Men.

This one could smell the stink of Hell on me. I was sure of it, the way it cackled and ran spryly, thinking I was one of *His* bounty hunters. Not me. And no, I'm not a zombie. I don't eat brains or have a hankering for flesh . . . not human flesh at least. I could murder a steak after a chase like this though.

The demon shifted into a panther the size of a Great Dane. Black as pitch, the thing scaled the wall of the dead-end alley I had cornered it in and climbed onto the roof of the building. I looked for another way to get to it and spotted the three-story construction droid again. Shaking my head, I started to dismiss it. The demon would avoid the droid—well, anything with enough steel in it. *Unless I make it climb.*

Pulling the Colt 1911 from my shoulder rig, I took a snap shot at the demon as it rushed along the roof. Giving it no place to come down, it took the bait and leapt onto the droid instead of taking a risk I'd hit it again with a silver slug. I spotted the inky form climbing up the large droid to avoid my bullets, zigzagging up the colossal struts of metal, hissing and screaming as it did. Iron wasn't something that could kill a demon, but it did cause it some burns. Lead and copper were useless. Silver usually did the job.

Usually. This bastard seemed to be able to deal with the slugs. The dagger wouldn't be enough to put it down. There were two ways to kill it. I could wait for the sun, which wasn't an option, or use the Colt in a different way. The Colt's arcane bite into my hand was torn away as I holstered it and started to climb the droid myself. This was stupid.

"The things you do for money, John," I said to myself. "The Nine Hells are you thinking?"

As I climbed, I could see parts of Dayside and the Barrier at the city center. The black and white wall that separated the two halves of Janus City glowed with a preternatural light. Always thought that was a weird thing. I also saw that the horizon was getting dangerously close to lightening.

Has it been five hours already?

Five hours of stalking the damn thing. Once contracted by the victim's widow, I'd been given a deadline of dawn. That was one reason I couldn't wait for the sun to weaken the demon enough for it to succumb to its injuries. Had it not been for the three grand, I might not have taken the contract.

Money made me do stupid things. And once put under contract, I followed through. I had to. I was bound to the signator for the length of the contract. *And the widow gave me until dawn.* Thought I'd get it handled easily, so I'd agreed. Here I was, hours later, regretting that poor decision.

Sunrise was coming. I felt it with a tug of the contract bound to my soul. I had to put this demon down before the sun rose or I'd lose more than money. My injured shoulder twinged as I climbed the damn droid. The phazen demon squealed and squawked, tasting my body's torment. Considering the gap between us, I didn't think I'd get to it before sunrise at this rate.

Enough of this. "Catch up!" I snarled.

In the blink of an eye, I was within arm's reach of the possessed man. One moment I was fifty feet from the demon, the next I was on top of it. My silvery blue ring faded to a dusky rose, its magic spent for the next week. It had done its job.

The skin of Clarence's hands and neck had sloughed off, revealing the black jet of the phazen demon's skin. The thing morphed back into a humanoid form, the face was a patchwork of Clarence's chalky white and the ember coals of the phazen demon's giggling face, like a flesh mask with burned holes where the demon's true face was revealed.

I grabbed the creature by the neck before it could act. The black, inky skin oozed around my fingers as they tightened, though the skin didn't burn me—which the phazen demon realized too late. *Creatures raised from Hell recognize their own.*

I squeezed harder and harder, bringing my gun's muzzle to the demon's forehead.

"Leave."

Its fear slipped for a second as it cackled again. "You already tried that, Gallic. I can't be hurt by your silver bullets. Not enough to matter," it said as it turned to look at the horizon where the dim flash of false dawn flickered.

"True. Maybe just leave and tell them below I hate them?" I thumbed the hammer of the 1911 .45 back.

"Never. I'm free once the sun rises." It smiled, Clarence's teeth stained by black ichor.

Shit.

"You're finished, Dead Man! Can't fulfill the contract. Guess who gets to play with you when you *do* get back?"

The cackle that followed drove icy daggers into my spine.

"Guess you get another hole in the head."

"How, Gallic?" the demon asked, still smiling, but the smile faltered as its nostrils flared. A scent that was like rotten eggs, but with something more maleficent underneath, rose around us.

"Oh, you caught that?" I asked, the sharp smell of brimstone filling my nostrils. There was an ember-like glow around my wrist that held the gun. The markings started to ripple and *clank* like chain links clattering together. The dark red light suffused the grip of my Colt, traveling up to the bullet in the chamber.

The demon wailed, trying to pull away from me. "You can't waste it on me. I'll go back, I promise. I promise. I—"

The rest of its response was cut short by the barking report of my pistol firing a silver bullet surrounded by a sliver of my soul energy through its cranium. The back of the demon's head exploded in black goo. The rest of the body deflated as the phazen demon's essence was blown out of the body of Clarence Goins.

The phazen demon was gone, driven back to Hell for punishment. Or to queue right back up and come torment anther soul in Janus City, for all I knew.

Bits of the black ichor hissing on my hand and face dissolved into black smoke and brimstone. A moment of vertigo swept over me after that shot. Goins's body threatened to fall from my nerveless fingers over the edge of the steel structure. Chastising myself for using too much, I leaned against the steel structure, pulling the body to my chest to keep it—and me—from falling. I needed the body for the money, and dropping it would ruin it more than it already had been.

Sliding down, I lay on my back. The steel rivets dug into my spine, but with Goins's dead, drained body in my arms, I finally took a satisfying breath.

"You're going to kill yourself one of these days. And you know who is waiting," a voice that sounded not unlike my ex, Moira, whispered in my ear.

"Yeah," I said to the empty air, smiling. "But I ain't there today."

Morgan's Pub

Once on the ground, I placed Goins's body in a body bag I had stashed in a tiny extradimensional pocket that I was allowed to access as a Dead Man. I'd learned rather quickly that it was always a good idea to try and keep one or two of these on hand. With some luck, I was able to hail, and somewhat threaten, a taxi driver to take me to the meeting place with speed. The park wasn't very far from the industrial park, but it was a close thing. He didn't even ask for money, yet I knew that it would come out of the three grand the widow owed me.

Goins's widow was there, waiting and weeping somewhat convincingly. I doubted she cried about Clarence. She was probably waiting for some life insurance thing. That would explain why she'd used me. Contracts, Dead Man contracts especially, were legally binding in Janus City to recover bodies that had been possessed.

"Brought him back," I said, setting the remains in the body bag down before her.

"Did he suffer?" she asked, sniffing.

"No," I said, trying to be convincing. It was a lie. Phazen demons burn the possessed souls out before wearing their bodies, but at least a part of Clarence's soul still survived somewhere in Purgatory, awaiting judgement.

"I'm glad," she said with a smile a little too quick and bright to be from a grieving widow.

Yeah, tell that lie sweetheart. I knew better, yet I didn't have a contract with anyone else to expose it. Not my issue.

She unzipped the bag before I could stop her and let out a gasp. "What is this?" the window asked, her face set in a sneer.

"Your husband."

"I contracted you to *free* him of the demon."

"I did." Taking a deep breath, I gave her a cold smile. "He's very free."

"He's dead, you asshole! I didn't—"

Her anger chilled the moment she looked into my eyes. I gave her my best smile, a rictus of a grin. She even flinched when I said, "You wanted him free. His soul is free. His body is free of his soul. Contract done."

"I hired you to—"

I pulled myself up to my full height and looked down at her. "You hired me? No, you *contracted* me to free him of the phazen demon that possessed him after death."

"This wasn't part of the contract."

I looked at the body and then at the woman again. She was pretty in black. "Why are you wearing black then? Expecting him to be found dead?"

"No," she said, looking at her dress. "It was just the first thing I threw on." She withdrew a cell from a hidden pocket in her dress. "I should demand an investigation by the new mayor! He's a personal friend of mine and Clarence's."

I slapped the cell phone out of her hand. "Think very carefully before you start calling 'people you know.'" There was a prickling of heat in the pit of my stomach. Yeah, I had killed Clarence. His widow had wanted me to do so. She couldn't come out and say it. Which is illegal, Can't hire a hitman. At least not in Janus City once Mayor Stanwick was finely ousted for corruption. Being as close as I was, I detected the harsh stink of demon magic on her. She might know a thing or two. Hells, she could've possessed Clarence with the phazen demon in the first place. But she didn't want to tangle with me or the Powers That Be and quibble about details. She seemed to sense my meaning and backed off, though she still glared at me.

"You killed my husband," she whispered.

"You contracted me to do it." I smiled.

"I hired you to free him—"

I raised my hand to stop her talking. "We'll be here for hours," I said, looking over my shoulder and seeing the creeping light of the sun. "I gotta go. You know how to pay me."

"I'm not going to pay you." She jerked her hand back and slapped me.

I stared at her as she winced, a wicked grin coming over my face. "Lady, you are *lucky* it's close to sunrise."

Her face fell, lips quivering. "What are you going to do?"

"Nothing, if you pay me," I said, letting the seconds drag by as I held her gaze. "Going to pay me?"

"Yes, I swear." Her body shrank in on itself as she broke eye contact, shivering a little.

"Good." I turned and started to walk away. I thought I saw her balk, yet she'd contracted me. If she wanted to remain in good standing, she'd get the money to my account. Once I left her, and thought I was far enough away from anyone spotting me, I bolted toward the nearest safe place, which was across the park and down a set of steps into a pub. I knew the owner. That was one reason I used the park, it was close to Morgan's.

I made it to the bottom of the steps just as the sun rose. My right hand had a small burn on it from holding onto the railing at the top of the stairs a touch too long as I steadied myself. Not really an issue. I'd heal up once I got some food in me and some sleep. Same with my strained shoulder and the slight burn on my hand from when I'd gripped the phazen demon.

One of the little curses I'd had thrust onto me because of being a Dead Man was I couldn't walk in the sunlight—a little loophole the Powers That Be of Janus City used to keep Dead Men in line. When I'm under contract, I can go wherever, day or night, even had carte blanche to go through the Gate to Nightside—though that was not a "privilege" I relished. With Clarence's widow releasing me with a promise of full payment, I'd had to leg it to stay out of the sun.

"John?" A rich feminine voice came from the darkened bar of the pub. A moment later, the sound of racking a shotgun round echoed through the pub. "That you?"

"Yeah, Morgan, it's me."

"You gave me a heart attack," Morgan said, flicking on a lamp. It illuminated a voluptuous woman with a mop of pale pink hair in an undercut. She was a Fae, and she glared at me. "What are you doing here? I didn't invite you in."

"I needed to get out of the sun. Plus, not a fanghead."

"And?" she asked, a dimple appearing on her right cheek, though still held the shotgun on me. It was an all-plastic model, only way she could have held it at all.

"You know I can't go into the sun."

"And?"

I sighed. Morgan's a friend. And a bitch at the same time. "Morgan, I'm here because—"

"None of that 'come for friendship' shite. Git out or pay up," she said, the shotgun never wavering.

I reached into my pocket and pulled out a fifty. "This is all I got."

The Fae took it, keeping the shotgun trained on me. She gave it a sniff. "It's deadmen money."

"The window didn't say he needed to have a full wallet. I lightened it a little."

"Yer a prick," Morgan said, finally letting the shotgun fall to her side.

"And your mead is the best in Janus City."

The Fae stopped when I said that. "Flattery will get you nowhere." She eyed me again for a moment, waiting for the other shoe.

"Can the fifty get me a pint?"

The Fae sneered at me for a long moment. Her bright neon blue polished thumbnail thumped against the grip of the shotgun a few times before she nodded. "Yes."

"Bitch." I lumbered closer.

"And? What's the magic word?" she asked, setting the shotgun aside, then plucked a mug down and filled it with a rich honey amber liquid. She held it out of reach until I said something.

"Still a better person than me. Please?"

"That's what I wanted to hear," she said while setting the mug down with a smile.

The mead was cool as it touched my lips, then warmed my insides. Felt like a drinking a sunny day. "Amazing as always."

"Thanks. Now, why are you here?"

"Told you, the sun was—"

Morgan shook her head. "None of that shite. Thought you had a place on the West Side with that little *sidhe*?"

"Nope."

Morgan waited a little longer. All I did was drink more of his mead. "Just a 'nope?' Nothing more?" Her eyebrows raised more, a glint coming off the golden hoop in her right eyebrow.

"You're right. Nothing more," I said, finishing the mead. "Have any food?"

"Rite bastard," she said before going to poke around for food.

"And?" I asked, hearing her give a small laugh.

No Rest for a Dead Man

Two hours and three meads later, Morgan had gone to get some sleep. She locked up the place and told me not to drink any more. *It's good to want things*, I thought while drinking the fourth mead.

The pub was filled with leather-covered bar stools and leather booths that took up the outer ring of the space, while seven tables sat scattered around the well-polished wooden floor. The only windows were at the south end of the bar and were made of a glass that allowed denizens of Janus City, even those from Nightside, stay and enjoy a little sun.

I refused to go to Nightside, the mirror of Dayside. Been there a few times and was not a fan. Nor was it safe to be a Dead Man in Nightside. Not for any length of time. You hear rumors of things that happen there to those like me who were given another chance for service to the city. Living in Nightside was not an option I wanted to think about.

Settled into one of the leather seats near the back of the bar, I ate the last of a platter of cold cuts and cheese Morgan had charged too much for. No bread. I don't like bread; sandwiches are lazy. Sitting down, enjoying the individual pieces of meat and cheese wrapped together, gave me time to think.

What was I gonna do now?

I'd taken $300 from Clarence's wallet when I put him in the body bag. There was still more that I could have taken, but three

Benjamins wasn't going to be missed. I'd lucked out that these were the old, old ones. I'd died on Earth about 2001or so, then went to Hell for reasons I don't want to get into. Then I'd ended up in Janus City and found that they'd changed the bills. I didn't like the new big, big face of Benjamin on it, or the color.

I couldn't rent a hotel room with the sun up. I could wait it out here until dusk, but I didn't like the idea of overstaying my welcome more than I had already. The best thing would be to be gone before Morgan woke up again.

I didn't have a place to crash partially because of my ex. It *had* been her place that I was crashing in, but still. *Damn Moira.* Never date a *sidhe. Bean sidhe* or otherwise. Still needed to get some of my stuff from that bitch. She had probably thrown it out on the lawn—or burned it. But there were two things she wouldn't find with the rest of her stuff, and if nothing else, getting those two items was crucial.

It'd still be a bitch and a half to do.

I licked the last crumbs of the cheddar from my fingers, not the yellow shite but the real cheddar cheese stuff from Jolly Olde Cheddar itself. This city is a bit of a weird metaphysical crossroads. People from all over who can get a second chance come here. And sometimes things come here as well. I didn't understand it all, but if Morgan had a hookup with actual cheddar, I was good with it.

I checked my hand. The sun burn was close to fully healed. A small slash of burned tissue across my knuckles was all that was left. Turning my hand over, another burn was right at the webbing of my thumb and forefinger that linked to the scar around my wrist, from the phantom chain that had pulled me up and bound me to Janus City. It would fade during the day, yet most denizens, and other Dead Men, could see it. When you burn part of your soul as a weapon, it has a cost.

I pulled the 1911 Colt out and took it apart by rote memory. It was a normal gun, except for the small bit on the grip. Right where it connected with the palm of my hand was a little rune that leeched out a little bit of my soul. No one can use my gun but me. Which I'm thankful for. It also acts as a conduit for the extra bit of power that my soul adds to the gun when I need it.

That power and the chain were the reminder of where I was before and who I worked for in Janus City. Not many people end up topside again, really. I woke from the endless suffering to see a chain dangling in front of me. Without thinking, I grabbed ahold and found myself given a choice. Home, to loved ones who had moved on, or to work for Janus City. It's obvious which I chose. It was the only place I felt comfortable, hell, the only place I *could* feel comfortable. The rest of the world had its own problems, so why would I want to show up on the doorstep of my parents or my old lover? I choose Janus City.

"Reminiscing?" a smooth and all too familiar voice asked. "In a place like this?"

Looking up from the disassembled gun, I found Mammon—the demon of Greed, a pale, ginger-haired man in a three-piece pinstripe suit seated across from me. He smiled, and there was a shine of a diamond in one of his eye teeth. He stroked his Van Dyke beard and looked at me and the pub.

"What can I say, I like living life a bit more low-key."

"Now, that isn't the John Gallic I remember," Mammon said. "You used to be so much . . ."

"Of a greedy pig?" I asked.

"You say that with such disdain. Really, John. I would have thought—"

"What do you want?"

"Simply to see how you're surviving up here in this crossroads," Mammon said, a bright smile on his face. "I really don't see how you could—"

"I'm getting by," I said. My hands moved on their own, reassembling the 1911 with more speed.

"You know, if you let me help you a bit, sponsor you more than as some latchkey gopher for these peasants here, I'm sure we could figure out something."

"I'm good, thanks."

Mammon rolled his eyes. "You were one of my finest while on Earth. And even in Hell, you were—"

"That's enough of that," I said, chambering a round into the Colt 1911 and pointing it at Mammon. "You can leave."

"Such violence," Mammon said. "Really, John. I—"

I pushed the Colt along the top of the wooden table until it touched Mammon's stomach. "I said, you can go."

"Very well, don't say I didn't warn you. I do hope you have fun trying to help the next unfortunate that contracts you, John Gallic."

He was gone in the blink of an eye.

Hate that guy.

Slipping the gun back into the shoulder holster, I let the comforting weight of the gun ground me in the moment.

Then a crash-thump crash-thump crash-thump came down the stairs in front of Morgan's place. The gun was out before I was out of the seat. A looming figure darkened the frosted glass of the front door. There was a moment of shock when a delicate knock-knock-knock on the wood sounded.

Intrigued, I went to investigate. I opened the door, finding a bear of a man reaching out for me. His eyes were rimmed with red as if he'd been crying for hours, and a rictus of pain twisted his lips. The oddest thing? He had one normal leg, one artificial one.

"They stole my leg!" the man shouted, reaching out to grab me by the shoulders. "They stole my leg!"

Moira

"I need you, John Gallic to find it!" the man screamed again.

"Relax, sir," I said, trying to be as diplomatic as possible.

"I have a contract right here," the man shouted again, shoving a thick rolled up piece of vellum into my hands. His right thumb still bled from sealing the contract moments ago.

The moment I touched it, I felt a tingle in my hand as if I held a live wire. Unfurling the vellum, I looked over the contract, feeling the subtle magic of the Powers That Be and their whims running over my skin and through me.

He'd given me a week to hunt down the one who took his flesh leg. It was legit, and with a final handshake, the deal was done. The moment he took my hand and shook it, a small sense of calm fell over him.

"Do you want to come inside?"

"No. No, I need to . . . I need to get back," he said, his eyes darting around the darkness of the pub's interior.

With him pausing, and no longer shouting at me to find his leg, I was able to get a better look at the new client, Kenneth Lang. Though I hadn't seen his name on the contract, it was burned into my mind the moment we shook hands. The subtle magic of the contract meant something else for me: I could leave the pub. Stepping out onto the front stoop of Morgan's Pub, I gave my new client a closer look.

The artificial leg drew my attention. It looked like a rush job some steamer had done, cobbling it together as if by committee. Made of many gears, with steam and oil leaking out, it reeked of grease and oil.

Overall, he looked like a stressed-out man in his thirties who could use a stiff drink. His body twitched a little, and he emitted small grunts of pain when he put too much weight on the artificial leg. The replacement leg's flywheels and gears chugged along, yet there was a widening pool of oil from somewhere as he stood there.

"You need to find my leg," Kenneth said.

"When did you see it last?" I asked, deadpan.

"When I woke up this morning, it was gone."

"Deal with gnomes, dwarves, or steamers?" I asked, hoping to find some connection.

"Who doesn't deal with steamers in this city?" he snarled. "I don't truck with any Fae if I don't have to."

He had a point. "Ken, I need you to relax and think—"

"Kenneth," he said.

I gritted my teeth. *One of those kinds of guys.* "Alright, *Kenneth*, relax. One last question. Have any dealings with gremlins?"

"Why?" he asked, head snapping up to glare at me as if I'd accused him of something wrong.

"Call it professional curiosity."

"Yes," he said after a moment. Next door neighbor's a gremlin. Has a small shop of some kind out behind his house, up at all hours with—"

"Let me deal with it. Please, go home. If I have any questions, I'll contact you."

"How?"

Never used a Dead Man before, huh? I tapped the vellum rolled up in my right hand. "This. You and I have a connection now. At any time, I can walk right to you no matter where you are in Janus City. You can do the same, it's how you found me. Though, I suggest you don't, unless I contact you and tell you to. Understood?"

"Yes," he grunted. "Just find my leg! Please! I need it!"

I plastered on my best smile. "Kenneth, I promise, I will find it. Relax, go home, and spend time with your daughter."

He sneered at me. "How do you know I have a daughter?"

I shrugged. It was part of the contract, but I didn't feel like explaining it again. "Lucky guess." I really wanted him to leave. He wanted me to find a leg, something that he should have felt gone the moment it was taken. Instead, he'd probably gotten steamers to cobble something together into a usable contraption. *This is gonna be a great day.*

"What in the Hell is going on?" Morgan shouted from inside the pub as Kenneth left up the stairs. "What are—"

I saw her coming toward the door, shotgun in hand and a sneer on her lips. I looked over and Kenneth was galumphing up the steps with his thump-crash thump-crash gait. Holding up my hands as I moved through the door, I gave her a smile. "Don't worry, I was just making a contract. I can leave now."

"Not until you clean up that oil," Morgan said, pointing at the pool of oil that Kenneth had left. I looked at the Fae and the Fae looked at me. For a moment, I thought about telling her to go spin. Then I remembered the contract that Kenneth had signed with a long lead time and a decent chunk of change. "You're right. Get a mop and bucket." At least I could do something that was a little bit of helping the client and pay back Morgan for some of the mead I'd drank.

CLEANING THE MESS HELPED me out in the end. There was something a bit odd and tougher to clean about it. I took one of the rags I'd used to sop up some of the oil and stuck it in my pocket. Once I got something from Moira's, I'd be able to track down who made it. I'm not just a pretty face.

After an hour of scrubbing, with the help of Morgan's cleaning charms, I was done. I gave her a nod. She nodded back as she drank her coffee-flavored whiskey, "Don't come back for a bit, please?"

"I promise to only try," I said with a beaming smile and left. I wanted to get to a guy I knew who sold parts of people. It's Janus City, so anything is possible here. The first thing I did was grab a cable car to Westside, where Moira lived. Before I dealt with anything, I needed my gear form Moira's vault.

As the cable car slid up along the hill of Westside, I looked back to see the dark gray area of Eastside. White stone of marble or plasterwork provided Westside a sharp contrast to the dark and ramshackle buildings of Eastside and thealternating black and white pillars of the Barrier, the massive wall that divided Nightside and Dayside. Not that there wasn't a night here or day there. But Nightside reminded me of London on a real foggy day with the sun out. Never burning the fog off, the sun still brightened the streets of Nightside enough to see without streetlamps.

The Powers That Be were strange with their city. Their whims were carried out by the mayor and, to a lesser extent, us Dead Men. They were the ones who imbued the contracts to work with the people of Janus City. So, if they ever wanted to end a contract, or extend one, they were the ones who did it.

That was one of the reasons people called this place Janus City there was a Day and Night side, one place always wreathed in darkness, the other having daylight. The duality of the place wasn't only in the stone of the city. Eastside wasn't the safest, yet it was better than Nightside. I was burning time to get to Moira's regardless, since there was a part of me that felt I was going to be dragged into Nightsider business with this leg theft.

From my vantage point on the cable car, I spotted the Central Square of Janus City and the Gate, a checkpoint of both sides of the city. Other gates and bridges had been built to get from one side of the city to the other. Yet, the main ingress was the Gate, a massive fifty-yard diameter portal of a perfect circle, half of it buried under the city. It cut into the center of the Barrier. There was a haze that always surrounded the yawning maw of the Gate. A slight illumination came from the lanterns and lights that surrounded the ring of the entrance, decorated with dozens of demonic and angelic faces and scenes of mythological creatures from every major religion of Earth. Plus a few that were bizarre and weren't from any history I knew. The rumors were that they were alien scenes of far-flung worlds of denizens that were yet to come to Janus City. Others said they were some far-flung future. Others said they were alternative histories, since at least one showed that Nazi shithead standing before the capitol of Washington with his little cartwheeling plus sign there.

Pissed me off whenever I saw it up close. As it did many others of the denizens close to the Barrier. Yet, no matter how many times people tried to deface it, the next day it would be repaired and looked brand new. As did any sculpture or carving that was defaced. The next dawn, it would be as if nothing happened to it.

I didn't know how it happened. No one wanted to know. Heard a rumor that a few drunks tried to stop it from being repaired one night. The next day, their faces were found to be in the crowd scene of the shithead. After that, people just ignored it.

I got off at Fifth and Hobart, then and made my way down the block and around the bank on the corner to see the Garren Arms Complex. When I rounded the corner, I felt a flash of anger flare up around my skin. A scent spiked in my nostrils, one I was familiar with.

Something was on fire.

The Vault

Rounding the corner of the Chase Bank across from Moira's apartment complex, the fire was apparent. It was on the front lawn of the Garren Arms. A woman in white with long flowing red tresses was laughing and drinking from some brightly colored martini glass, it looked like. It was Moira, dancing around a small pile of boxes on fire. Each had my full name, JOHN GALLIC in big black marker scrawled on the sides.

Names have power, and Moira had inadvertently—at least I hoped—set something on fire with my name on it. Hence the flash of heat on my skin. If I hadn't been on a contract, I'm not sure I would've been able to walk up to her as she laughed, drank, and let out whoops of joy.

"Moira!" I shouted, making her turn around.

When she did, the grin she gave me was cold, and her eyes blazed with an inner green flame that caused a part of me to tremble. Other parts did other things. She was lovely and terrifying. What can I say, I have a type.

She was a shade under five foot seven, with long straight red hair that hung to her mid-thigh. Her bright green eyes devoured me, lit up with a joyful anger. Her pale, near-translucent skin changed subtly when she realized I was so close to her. The *sidhe* coming out. Her hair changed to a pale pink, while a deathly pallor came over her skin. Her eyes shone even brighter.

"Well, look who finally returned," Moira said, a bright-colored martini in one hand, the other on her hip. Her wrists swam with bangles of gold and silver, floating and shifting along her wrists in subtle patterns. Her smile grew more predatory as she took a long sip of her drink.

"Thanks for the warm welcome." I walked past her, not seeing how the barb landed. "Got something in your apartment."

"Everything of yours is there," she said, moving with speed and grace to slip in front of me while pointing toward the small fire. "Can't go in anyway, you aren't invited."

"Not everything." I said, giving her a wink before continuing toward the front door and the slab of humanoid stone that guarded the entrance.

I heard her shout my name, a small twinge plucking at my soul. I might be quasi-undead, yet when a *bean sidhe*shouts your name, even Dead Men feel something. She said it again, and the twinge turned to an icy dagger.

"What?" I snarled, turning to look at her.

"Tole ya, I gathered everything," Moira said, gesturing with her drink to the boxes, which were mostly blackened ruins. Her drink slopped out. *Probably not her first.*

"Stuff in the vault?" I asked.

Her face, her entire body, snapped back to the pale flesh and red tresses, her eyes losing some of their fire. She arched an eyebrow. They were back to their darker red shade too. "You don't have the combo to that."

Before I turned toward the front door again, I mouthed the first two digits to her. I might be a jerk, but I wasn't going to announce her vault combo to the world at large. Shaken, she took an involuntary step back as I continued toward the door.

"Fuck you, Johnnie." In the blink of an eye, she was in front of me again. The martini glass stem in her hand snapped as she crushed it in her hand. With her free hand, she slapped me hard across the face, then let out a hiss of pain from the strike.

"Not now, I'm on a job," I said with a smirk. Seeing the barb hit, I turned to stare at the giant stone golem. Portal. Most of the golems who guarded the entrance to doorways in Janus City had some name like Gate or Portal or something.

"Mr. Gallic, I am sorry, but you are not allowed inside," the voice was gentle, firm, and polite. The impassive face of the humanoid form stared down at me.

"Gate, I gotta go in and fetch something. My property's in there."

"But it is in her vault, isn't it?" Gate asked, looking at Moira for confirmation, then myself. "You are not allowed."

I had to be careful. Gate was a Fae. They had weird feelings about possession.

Something came to mind, and I thought I'd take a chance. "It's soulbound to me, though."

He pondered my words for a moment. His all-yellow eyes glowed for a moment as he contemplated what I'd said. He nodded, his body making a grinding noise of stone on stone, and opened the door. "You are granted a one-time admittance."

"Thanks Gate. Say hey to the wife and kids."

Gate nodded, and even a ghost of a smile showed on his broad face. "Thank you, sir."

Moira stayed hot on my heels, trying to scream and swear at me. She kept saying my name. Each time she did, an icy dagger drove deeper into the very core of my being. My hands kept opening and closing, wanting to commit serious violence. As she stopped me at the elevator, the door opened and a gaggle of goblins bounced out and around us, tittering and laughing. The biggest one, the mother of the brood, held onto two tiny, swaddled goblin babies and cursed as the children and their beleaguered father moved out of the elevator. "Jess, please restrain *your* children!"

"They are *our* children, harpy!" The tallest male squawked back, yet ducked as the goblin mother swung at him with a baby. Then, they all spotted Moira and I and grew very quiet before pushing their children toward the door.

The mother shouted out, "We simply *must* have coffee sometime soon, Moira *darling*!"

"Very soon, Mrs. Kolbinik," Moira said in a near whisper as she lunged into the elevator after me.

"Johnnie," Moira started.

The dagger stabbed hard, making me gasp. "That's it!" Grabbing her by the shoulders, I leaned down a little to look into her eyes and pulled her closer. "I'm not going to hit you. But *stop* saying my name, you damn harpy."

That word stopped her dead. "Do I look like a saggy-titted has-been bird to you? The audacity!" Her lips curled in a genuine grin.

"No. Still a fiery beauty. You're going to kill me by degrees if you keep it up," I whispered back, leaning in closer. The scent of apples and booze, along with her floral perfume, made me lean in closer.

Spotting the smile on her face, I smirked back.

"Maybe that's what I wanted. Mayhaps you deserve to die, ya focking prick." She didn't struggle out of my grip, only glaring up at me with her fierce green eyes.

"Missed you too," I whispered, moving in closer to kiss her. Then stopped. "But I'm on a case."

"As always," she hissed. Pulling away from me, she slapped me hard across the face. "Gods great and small, I want to blast your soul apart." Again, she winced at hitting me so hard.

When she tried to slap me again, I grabbed her hand and pressed close to her. "Tell me something I don't know."

"I still love you." Her hands wrapped around my head, yanking me in for a hard kiss. She then bit my lower lip, pulling away and holding the moment for a heartbeat. Then she shoved me backwards. "You prick."

The elevator door dinged open, and she sashayed away while I stood there, dumbstruck for a moment. I shook my head free of the cloud of perfume and followed after her, whispering, "This is a big fucking mistake."

On the Trail

Still shaking from Moira's confession, I followed her to her door. She seemed to have resigned herself to me coming back into her place one more time. "Please tell me you didn't burn the Poe books?" I asked as she touched the doorknob.

She turned and looked at me. "I gave those to you. They're expensive. I'm pissed at you, not insane. I'm keeping them," she said as the door opened on soundless hinges.

I let out a small sigh of relief as I followed. Then I hit the threshold of her apartment and was violently shoved backwards. "You re-cast your threshold ward against me?"

"What are you going to do? Cross the threshold uninvited?" she asked as she cocked her head to the side, a mischievous grin on her face.

If I did, I'd lose much of the protections I had as an undead. I'd be near human, weak as a kitten and stuck in an apartment with a *sidhe* who hated me. *But she loves you,* a stray thought came to me. *Yeah, issue is she loves me but wouldn't mind flaying the skin from my bones for the fun of it.*

"Well?" she asked, looking at me, her green eyes kindled with that same joyous anger. Her smile touched her eyes in a wicked way. She was daring me to try it.

"Never dare me," I said. She'd have an intense advantage over me if I did so, but I had to get my things. Gritting my teeth, I stepped toward her. Immediately, the pressure of the threshold latched onto me as if chains of protection wrapped tight around my chest, legs, arms, and even around my neck. A slight green ephemeral glow sprang to life from the chains, weighing me down more and more, pulling at the protections of my undead status. Moments later, I tore them apart, staggering against the wall, gasping for air and sweating copiously. The Powers That Be liked to make sure people felt as safe as they could. Threshold wards were to protect people from various supernatural things, even Dead Men. One of these days, I wanted to try and get an audience with the Powers, find out who they were and why they'd set up the rules they did. *That* was a pipedream. No one spoke to the Powers, except maybe the mayor. And even that was a stretch to say. More like he spoke *at* them.

"Was it really worth it?" she asked, taking a sip from some concoction in a highball glass and pulling me from my wayward thoughts.

I shook my head, snatched the glass from her, and slammed the contents down in a single gulp. I felt the harsh burn of Moira's favorite, a bitter sour mixer with whiskey, all the way down.

"Thanks, Moya," I said, handing her the empty glass. Looking around the apartment, it hadn't changed much. A bit cleaner without some of my clothes and books no longer scattered about. There was a leather and brass trimmed sofa, a loveseat, end tables, and a few other things that screamed luxury. With her work at the Chase Bank across the street, she could afford it.

A small vein throbbed on her forehead. "I hate that name."

I ignored her and walked toward the wall where her vault access was. I raised my hand as I neared the picture of one of her relatives. It faded to nothing. A light blue combination dial the size of a softball appeared in its stead where the two-foot-square door of the same color waited. The dial spun around a half dozen times back and forth randomly, then settled on "00," waiting.

With a few flicks of my finger, the dial spun to the different numbers in the combination. The vault itself is an extra-dimensional bank box that everyone in Janus City has access to. Everyone gets their own combination when they register as a citizen. I'd been given one as a Dead Man. One reason I'd shacked up with Moira was she had a decent account and I was able to get a small pocket vault without her knowing. It wasn't as hard as I'd expected. And yes, I'm a scumbag for doing it. Never said I was a good person.

The door popped open, and Moira gasped when she saw the near-empty vault.

"Relax, this is mine, not yours," I said. I had used Moira's since I wanted to keep the two items in the stash in a more secure place, since I didn't fully trust my Dead Man account, not fully.

Reaching in, I pulled out the two items I'd stored inside: an enchanted long coat that was better than most kinds of armor and pair of ensorcelled sunglasses that helped me track down my signatories. And other targets, with the right ingredients.

"You used my vault to store your junk?" Moira shouted.

"It isn't junk," I said, pulling on the long coat. Her anger caused a small throb in my soul. Slipping on the sunglasses, I smirked. "I need these to do my job." The glasses wouldn't solve the case for me, but they were ensorcelled to show a path to anything I touched to them and whispered the right words. And I *should* be able to see what I was walking toward if the glasses still worked the way they were suppose too. I hadn't used them in some time, since I'd been booted out of Moira's two weeks ago.

"You know I could scream and kill you?" she asked, another one of her highballs already in hand.

I smirked at her. With the glasses, I could also see any kind of arcane build up. There was none. Even a *sidhe* needs a few moments to build up that power. I walked closer to her, looming over her. She stood her ground, scowling at me. I shook my head. "Doubt it, Moira. You love me, remember." I then placed a kiss on the top of her forehead. Her scowl disappeared into a blank mask as I left.

Walking out of the apartment was an invigorating rush as the chains slipped over me again, this time pushing the power of a Dead Man back into me. As my hands and body stopped trembling from the loss of power, I wondered what would have happened had Moira followed through on her threat. I was a contractor to someone in Janus City, I'd come back . . . somehow.

Hearing a shuffle of movement, I looked back to see Moira standing in the doorway. She whispered something as I turned the corner toward the elevator. Not sure if she meant for me to hear it, but I had pretty good hearing.

"Don't die, ya big lug."

I didn't respond until I was in the elevator, far away from her. I looked back toward where she would be standing, "I'll try Moya, I'll try."

WHILE THE ELEVATOR descended, I shook off the tension that had built up. When the door opened, I entered the lobby and was assaulted by Gate appearing in front of me from nowhere.

"Did you retrieve your items?" he asked in his monotone rock grinding voice.

"Yeah, I'm leaving. Promise." I said, still distracted from what had happened in the apartment and his being right there.

"I ask you not return until and unless Ms. Moira invites you."

"Or I have a client who lives here," I said, giving Gate a small smile.

"Yes . . . sir." The golem didn't seem certain, yet didn't see anything I said was false either. Still, he didn't look at me with any sympathy.

Seeing that I had pushed as far as I could with the golem, I saluted him and walked away.

I turned to business. Finding Kenneth's leg. With that thought, I felt a strange tug to move away from the apartments and start moving down a side street. I followed it, not even sure what I was doing. In my head, I was trying to figure out who would take a leg and leave someone high and dry.

"How'd he sleep through it?" I asked myself.

"I'm sorry?" a female jogger asked, looking at me like I was crazy as she waited for a chance to cross the street.

"Sorry, I was thinking out loud."

She turned up her nose at me and kept on jogging as soon as she could. I tried to not look like I was watching her jog away, but at the same time, I was wearing shades and it was rather easy to watch the girl with the orange sports bra jog away from me.

From the corner of my eye, I saw a dark shroud skimming toward me. Before I could react, I was plunged into a black, inky void and a rough gravelly voice whispered in my ear, "Stop what you're doing, or you won't survive the next twenty-four hours."

Heavy

A hard fist struck me square in the face. I spit blood into the sack over my head. I was protected by the Powers That Be, yet I still felt it.

"Do you understand?" the rough whisper asked.

"Yeah," I muttered, the coppery tang in my mouth still tingling my tongue.

"Good," the voice said with a touch of happiness.

Before I could answer, I was shoved out of whatever moving vehicle I was in, hitting a patch of asphalt and rolling a few times. I ripped off the enchanted hood, finding myself still in the Westside of Dayside, but closer to the Barrier than before.

Not wanting to spend more time than I had to in Westside, I headed toward a cable car stop and hopped on one of the green cars when it slid to a stop. One good thing about the cable cars was the price. Anyone could ride in Janus City for free. One of the few perks of the city, unlike Frisco or L.A. The Janus City cable cars worked off the inherent magic of the city itself. It wasn't always a good thing to have random bits of magic streaming through the air. Most of the homes that faced a cable car road were shod with cold iron or had magic rods of silver along the sides to catch and ground the energy—or dissipate in the case of the cold iron.

Hopping on, I noticed I was alone except for the driver and an elf. The elf sat by himself—or herself, you never know with the Fae. And this elf was one of the "heavies." The elf had become part of Janus City's reality, like Moira or Morgan. Morgan and Moira could head back to the Fae Realm, the Fade, whenever they wanted. Both of them would prefer being dragged over a mile of broken glass, on their stomachs, than ever going back and dealing with the Shadow Court. From what little Moira had said, it made American politics looks like a child's game. Families, lineages, were set up, rose to power, or died in the complex machinations of the Shadow Court. With Oberon dead and Tatania gone to parts unknown, it was a savage place. I figured there were reasons Morgan never talked about it. I'd never pushed her.

I didn't blame either of them for wanting to stay on this side of the Fade, either. Elves—like the one sitting across from me, had grown "heavy," deciding to stay in Janus City while turning their backs on the Fade and the Shadow Court completely. The consequence of it was they could never return to the Fade, ever. Sometimes, they ended up looking like this guy, poor sod. Disconnected from their world but unable to deal with this one because they didn't understand it, they wasted away. About ninety pounds soaking wet, he was clad in an ill-fitting suit at least two sizes too big as if he'd withered more and more.

After a few moments, the elf glanced up at me, trying to shrink into the bench more. His eyes were sunken with dark circles underneath. He shook as I looked at him. For a moment, something didn't register. Not until I realized my shades were still on and the elf had an orange-hued aura surround him. He was connected to Kenneth and his missing leg.

As he watched me with his sunken eyes, I moved a bit closer to him, making him break eye contact. It was just him and me—and the automaton driver, who might as well have been part of the car with the way the cable cars worked. Yet some regs stated there had to be a "driver" of some kind with an intelligence.

"Nice day," I said to the elf.

He said nothing, just continued to stare into the middle distance between us. But he did inch away from me while trying to sink deeper into the bench seat. That's when I caught an odd odor coming from him. Most Fae, even heavies, smell of fields, grass, and the wilds. Moira had a scent of rich soil and withering flowers when she didn't wear something to mask it. The heavy reeked of the docks and dying fish.

"Hey, buddy, I'm talking to you." I reached out to poke him in the leg.

When I touched him, two things happened: First, he let out a keening that caused me to grit my teeth and wince. The high-pitched scream dug into my ear drums like rusty nails. Second, he collapsed onto the floor of the cable car, starting to thrash about from a sudden a seizure. Dropping beside him, I pulled out my wallet to jam it between his clenching teeth so he didn't bite his tongue off. His eyes grew more unfocused as the seizure crashed through him. He bit down so hard on my wallet, it started to bend.

"Dammit, stop this thing! Call emergency services!" I shouted out at the automaton.

The cable car was already slowing when I shouted. The thing's big metal head turned and looked at me. The face, painted on over a glowing speaker for a mouth, lit up as it said in a crackling monotone, "Emergency services have been summoned, please remain calm." The words continued over and over in a loop.

One of the elf's hands grabbed my forearm. He spat out my wallet and hissed out, "Quetzal . . ." His voice faded as his eyes closed and his body went still. Being a Dead Man, I watched his spirit leave the body. A fading greenish blue spirit of the elf stared down at his body, then at me, shocked that I was staring right at him. It shrugged a little and started to fade. I dug into my pocket for a ghost trap, then cursed, realizing Moira had burned them all.

One last shot. I started to mumble out the one incantation that I knew to stop spirits from departing. It was a perk of the job. The chain scar around my wrist started to rattle and clank as it writhed on my wrist. A spectral, red-hued chain slipped from my hand toward the spirit. It touched the elf spirit, and there was a flare of pain.

The energy of the spell snapped back on me. With a hiss, I snagged the chain before it flailed around more. The elf spirit disappeared in hiss of steam. That wasn't normal. Pain flared in my chest when the chain made contact. Touching the burn, I felt heat still coming off it.

"Shit, the ghost was bound to someone, body and soul," I muttered to myself. The burn was a perfect circle, I knew. The runes that had tried to form a death curse had fallen apart when they touched my skin to bind to me. A Janus City contract is more powerful. Overrides pretty much anything. One of the few perks to being a contractor for Janus City was that I was protected.

However, the heavy had given me something to follow up on. I had to see Quet now, the feathered serpent of death.

Wraith

"Why is it when there's a weird death, you're always close by, Johnnie?" Detective Vince Chung asked, looking up from his notepad, a sneer on his thin, angular face. His pencil didn't shift much while I gave him the gist of what had happened. The glances he shot my way gave me some hope he believed it. He kept giving a sidelong glance at his partner and then me, once and again. He was a skinny guy, vaguely Asian and a thin wisp of facile hair on his lip. Like someone had rubbed his lip in dirt.

"Working on a case, Vin. Stumbled onto the heavy. Poked him 'cause he had something to do with the case. He had a seizure and croaked it right there."

"Uh huh." Vince glanced up at me again. Then his partner.

She shook her head as she walked over from talking with the driver.

"What he means is," Detective Elissa Montez—Vin's voluptuous wife—asked, coming up beside me. "Why are you in Westside?"

I looked over at her. She flashed me an easy, perfect white smile, one she knew I still liked. About six months ago, she and I had had a weekend together. A fling, nothing more. She'd needed a distraction, and she's easy on the eye. Her mixed heritage showed in her dusky skin, thick lips, olive-green eyes and spicy nature. She'd gone back to her husband Vince without a backward glance, as agreed. I'm sure he knew about our tryst, but he hadn't done or said anything about it.

Yet.

"If you gotta know, I was visiting the ex." I pushed the glasses up my nose. "Getting a few things I left there after I was asked to leave. I'm on a case, so can we wrap this up?"

"She didn't torch something of yours?" Vince asked, a small smirk on his face. The wisp of a moustache on his face made him look creepier and more pathetic than usual.

"Funny," I said, glaring at Vince. "I tried to help the heavy, alright? I gotta go." It wasn't that I felt nothing for the elf. It's a rough life. But this case I had was what I needed to focus on, not why some heavy Fae had died when I touched him. I needed to track down a lead with these glasses. Whatever the elf's connection to the case was, it wasn't good. The name he'd dropped worried me more, if I'm being honest.

"Not yet. Need to come with us to headquarters," Elissa said, touching my arm lightly. Chung cocked an eyebrow at her, though he stayed quiet.

"Why?" I raised an eyebrow. "What's the charge? Am I being detained?"

"Whoa, whoa," Vince said. His hands came up to touch Elissa's hand.

She moved her hand away from my arm before he did. "Nothing like that, Johnnie. No, we aren't detaining you. How about you go, just give us your cell?"

"Don't believe in 'em," I said. It wasn't that I didn't. I just had a habit of forgetting them and crushing them when I sat down. Or getting pissed off at who I was talking to and crushing them in my hand. Or they'd get hexed by damn magic-flinging people.

Magic and tech didn't blend well. Yet, cell companies tried to make advances to keep their customers happy here in Janus City. Few people in Janus City used them. They were outright illegal in Nightside. Though, there's a thriving black market for them there.

"I've gotta a burner you can hold onto for a bit," Elissa said. She walked away from us, her hips swaying from side to side in that seductive way. Both Vince and I enjoyed the view as she went to the squad car and leaned in through the passenger-side door to retrieve the cell.

I pulled my eyes away from her when Vince turned to ask me something. I didn't catch it at first—my mind was elsewhere.

"Huh?" Movement caught my eye, and I looked to see the body of the Fae slipped into the back of the black Medical Examiner's van. The M.E. smiled at me. He always had a permanent smile plastered on his false face. He had to have a painted wooden mask on, since he didn't have an actual face. I have no idea what happened to it, or if he was even born with one. Nice guy overall, for a face stealer. He didn't do that anymore to anyone living. Working for the Janus City PD helped him keep that wooden and metal thing bolted onto his face. I had a feeling that the elf wouldn't get more than a cursory look before being tossed into a potter's field without a face. That was the trade-off. Can't steal the face of anyone living, but he can peel one off any corpse he worked on.

"When did you stop fucking my wife?"

I snapped my head back to Vince. *Shit.* "I don't know what you're talking about." The lie came out with ease.

There was a moment of hesitation as Vince's eyes tightened. Leaning in close, he whispered, "I let the first weekend last year slide, Johnnie. But the last two months? Not cool. Stop fucking her. She's my *wife*!" The last words were said through clenched teeth. As Elissa moved closer, he smiled at her while she slipped the burner phone into my hand.

"You two alright?" she asked, glancing between the two of us, a look of concern passing over her beaming face.

"Fine," I said, giving her a smile and taking the sleek little phone. The contact of her skin on mine was electric. Then I blinked because the phone flared with an orange light when viewed through the ensorcelled glasses I still wore.

"Good, we're done here." Vince said, taking Elissa by the elbow and guiding her toward the car again. He looked over his shoulder, shooting a glare at me.

I needed to clear my head. As I walked away, my eyes kept going to the phone in my hand. After walking well away from the scene, and getting into a more commercial area of Dayside, I grabbed some wall in an alley to get a closer look at it.

It was an old school flip phone. Images of the original *Star Trek* show came to mind as I flicked the phone open. A small note fluttered out. Grabbing hold of it before it hit the ground, I recognized Elissa's handwriting. It was a phone number and four words in her loopy hand. "I need your help."

STARING AT THE NOTE, I was at a loss. Calling her then wasn't the right move. She and Vince would be together. I'd call after I resolved this this mess with Kenneth and his leg. Folding the note back, then pushing the cell into my pocket, I continued to follow the trail of the glasses.

Touching the glasses focused them. A very faint glow emerged from the city center. I hadn't noticed it before. Since I was closer and able to adjust the glasses a bit more, I judged from the softer glow that it was Morgan's place. The trail started to get brighter, merging with other trails as I moved closer to the city center. Following the trail from Morgan's, it joined the larger trail moving toward the Barrier.

Strolling along the streets of Westside toward the Barrier got me the usual dirty looks from the people who lived here. They were mostly humans, a handful of demons, angels, and Fae who gave me especially dirty looks or tried to hide their kids.

Fuck 'em. Let 'em gawk. Dressed in a shabby coat and pants, a walking corpse-like Dead Man stuck out. I didn't want to look to directly at the surrounding denizens. Angels and demons had magic to conceal what they looked like. Angles were things made of fire, eyes, and wings. Not something I wanted to let my mind grapple with at the moment.

Getting closer to the Barrier, a section of black basalt-like stone marked the sudden end of Main Street. The glowing trail bent to the right.

A chill swept over me as I saw I was close to a section of the Barrier known to have smaller passages and warrens burrowing though it into Nightside. I was so focused on following the trail that I didn't notice until it was too late that someone was tailing me. I happened to catch my reflection out of the corner of my eye in the large display window of the Gimble's department store and spotted a lurking form close on my heels. It wasn't a man or woman, only a shadow. I wasn't sure if it was real or a trick of light, but my gut made me turn to confront my pursuer.

I wasn't prepared to come face to face with the green-flame-wreathed face of a Wraith. Wraiths are the guardians of the Barrier. They are supreme dicks with *zero* sense of humor. They also just so happen to loathe the recently resurrected, like myself.

"What are you doing here, thing?" the voice hissed in my brain like a buzzsaw. To them, I'm an abomination, someone who escaped the Underworld and therefore my just punishment. Part of the Barrier manifested in the Underworld, as did these guardians. Glancing around, I realized no one could see this interaction. The Wraith and I had somehow become alone on the busiest street in the city. With my shades, I caught the edge of a spell boundary that surrounded the Wraith and me in a dome of avoidance.

Fan-fucking-tasctic.

"Following a clue," I said, touching my glasses to tamp down their ability. I didn't need to see more than the surface of the shroud. *Not again.* "We have an issue?" I asked without a tremor, proud of myself.

"You are not allowed here, abomination."

I tapped my temple. "Wrong. I'm on the clock, Guardian. I'm on contract. Have full authority within Janus City." It was a shaky leg to stand on, since the closer one got to the Barrier, it was less Janus City than it was the Barrier. It had its own rules, which interacted with the two sides of Janus in odd ways. *Fucking Wraiths.*

"You are close to being outside your jurisdiction, abomination," it said, the words causing an ache behind my eyes and a building pressure in my ears. It slithered closer to me. Close enough to see the green flames of its eyes and the faint green outline of its skull. "Be quick about your business and leave this area. Dead Man."

The last few words rattled around in my head. Something I was doing was bothering the Wraiths? Of all the collected peoples of Janus City, the *fucking Wraiths of the Barrier* were pissed at me.

Terrific. Fucking terrific. Greatest day of my second life.

I needed a drink, a smoke, and a fuck. But none of those were happening anytime soon. Not until I got to the bottom of this case.

There are some days I wished I had stayed dead.

Quet's

With a pulse of light, the glowing trail pulled my attention away from the Wraith for a heartbeat. When I turned back, it was gone. "Good riddance," I muttered to myself. The trail had changed to a blue-green, which meant I was at the start of the trail for the day.

"Why would he be around here?" I asked myself as I looked around.

The trail led toward a section of the City Center I'd been to more than once. It was also close to a shop owned by one Quetzalcoatl, formally the feathered serpent god.

Quet's place was closer to his own little section of the Barrier. The serpent god had fallen on hard times without anyone giving him ritual sacrifices. Looking at the Barrier, there was a split between a white and black section. Different versions of a half dozen death gods carved and etched into the massive white and black parts. I picked out the section that was Quet's. There he stood in his ancient glory, grasping a bleeding heart and holding it aloft like a prize as the blood trickled down into his open snake-like mouth. I thought I had gotten to who had taken Kenneth's leg.

I'd met the one-time deity while on another case. He had been very pleased to announce who he was and what he was—and the little side hustle that kept him in blood and body parts.

Harvesting.

In Janus City, plenty of things besides *baen sidhe* and elves lived. More malevolent things. Creatures that needed blood to live or happened to like the flesh of humans. And Quet had made a bit of a reputation for himself for being one of the top-end harvesters of people in Janus City.

His shop looked closed. It was supposed to be a "rejuvenation" center for those who wanted a ten minute or hour massage. Yet, it was more of a clinic for whatever quackery could be peddled. Snake oil salesmen, a staple when I was on Earth, were alive and well here on infomercials and at these kinds of "rejuvenation health spa" sites.

The backside of Quet's "clinic" faced a large alley for deliveries to the varied businesses that were up and down the street. I sneaked along a smaller side alley, but when I peeked around the corner toward Quet's, something was strange. The back door was fully open and it reeked like a charnel house.

Gun out, I moved fast and came in hot. Sweeping the barrel from one side of the open bay to the other, I took in a scene of carnage. Quet lay across a metal bench, broke and bleeding. Blood, body parts, even another heavy elf were strewn around the back workshop of his harvesting side hustle. Moving to Quet, as I reached out to find a pulse, he looked up at me. One eye was swollen closed, the other threatening to close as well. Gasping for air, he gave me a wet hacking chortle.

"John Gallic? Why are you here, Dead Man? Come to finish the job?"

Something about his words made me look more closely at his gaping mouth. His pronounced snout hung open to reveal two bleeding holes where someone had ripped out his fangs.

"Who did this?" I asked.

Quet mumbled something, but I wasn't sure what he said. He gasped for breath and hacked up more blood. He grabbed a piece of parchment and wrote with his own blood the words, "Warehouse 10. Before sundown," before his head dropped.

I took the parchment, not sure what I could do for him. He was still breathing, yet it might not continue if he wasn't helped soon. Quet didn't look good. Part of me knew I should wait. Then I looked outside, and judging from the slant of the sun, sundown was coming. I didn't have time to wait around. *Shit.*

I pulled out the cell Elissa had given me. I thought about calling the precinct and leaving an anonymous tip. At that moment, the phone went off. Elissa's name appeared on the screen of the flip phone.

"Elissa, I—"

"John, where are you?"

"Near the Barrier, near Warehouse Ten," I said while shoving the parchment into my pocket.

"Stay there. There are units en route close by. There were shots fired at Quet's place."

Fuck! "That's where I am, Elissa. I'll be careful."

"You're gonna have to explain some things," she said. "Like—"

I hung up on her, then turned off the cell. I didn't ditch it, just shoved it back into my pants pocket and raced out the door.

I had to regroup, and I needed to talk to Kenneth. I had to know how he was connected to Quet. How'd a supposedly normal guy get involved in this shit? Still walking along the side alley, I slipped on my tracking sunglasses again. Touching them, the trail I'd followed grew brighter. That meant I was within a quarter mile of my target.

I realized then that Kenneth wasn't the "normal" citizen he'd claimed to be. Yet, if he was dealing with Quet, that wasn't a shock.

"Should've taken my advice, prick," I muttered to myself as I moved. I looked in the shop and saw that a trace of green-blue was smeared along the wall and the door at the back of the shop.

"The leg was here?" I looked back at Quet's. I shook my head, thinking of what the cops would find when they got there. "You'll be happy to wake up, even though it'll be under arrest."

I continued to follow the trail toward the warehouse district.

Dead Men

The warehouse district was an amalgam of low-slung buildings that abutted the Barrier. Some people used them for workspaces, others for storage, and some squatters used them for shelter. The one the trackers led me to was once a pharmacy front. Kenneth's leg was in there, or it should've been. My hand strayed to my shoulder rig for a second to comfort myself more than anything.

As I moved closer, the first few drops of rain splattered down. It started as a gentle shower but turned to a heavier rain in a matter of moments. While annoying, it didn't stop me from continuing to move closer and closer to the abandoned drugstore. The storefront had large boards nailed up to cover up where the glass windows had been. A rusted metal gate hung partially open between the two boarded-up sections of the storefront. The faded outline of an ancient Rexall Drugs sign sat above the storefront. I was sure another would pop up somewhere in Janus City at some point. *Nothing stays dead in Janus City, for the right price.*

Standing before the gate, I realized it had been forced open and shrugged my shoulders to feel the weight of the pistol again. The smell of rain and wet concrete permeated the air. The drooping chains and broken lock caused the gate to look ajar. Pushing through without a further thought, I stood in the broken entrance, peering into the gloom of the store.

When my hand touched the door, the glow flared for a moment in the store. *I'm on the right track.* I yanked open the door with a grin, ready to end this case.

Two bullets zinged by me, slamming into the doorframe and flinging chips of wood toward me. Dropping into a crouch, gun already out, the burning and rippling thrum of the runes in my wrist already clanged away. This wasn't the time for half measures. I fired off a shot, fueled with a bit of my soul, in the direction of the shots. The bullet glowed a dull red, a reflection of the runes circling my wrist. The light wasn't enough to cut through the gloom. The slug struck an empty shelf with a brief flare of light. From the darkness came the sound of shuffling running feet, then the sound of a door banging open. A bright rectangle of light framed the fleeing form. Firing off another quick shot, I missed the form by an inch as the figure escaped into the lit storage area.

The glasses had switched off completely the moment I pulled my gun. With the danger gone, they flickered on for a few seconds. The glasses interacted strangely with the runes on my wrist. I never understood it properly and didn't think there was a wizard around who would give me a straight answer—or know one who told the truth. Glad the glasses had learned their lesson about the gun, I followed the deep blue-green glowing footsteps toward the fleeing person. That caused a moment's pause. Whoever it was had two legs, yet the glasses were keyed to Kenneth. "Well at least this will be answered in a moment," I muttered to myself.

I charged toward the door, gun leading the way. I swept right to left, dropping to one knee as I swept to the left around the door. Good thing too, since whoever I was chasing fired at where my head should have been. Reacting without thought, I slammed the muzzle of my gun into the guy's stomach. It took every ounce of willpower to not pull the trigger and end this.

The form grunted and doubled over. Helped by his momentum, I yanked him down while I covered him. Slamming him face first onto the concrete floor, I knelt on his back, pressing my gun's muzzle to the back of his head.

"No wait, don't shoot," the man shouted. His very familiar voice caused me to hesitate.

When I pulled the muzzle back from the guy's shaggy dark head, he turned toward me. It was my client, Kenneth.

"I told you to stay home, you dumb twat." I stood up and frowned down at him, looking him over as he pushed himself to his feet. That was when I realized he had two normal legs. I pointed my gun at him again. "Who are you?"

"I'm Kenneth, your client," he said while arching an eyebrow and twisting his lip in a sneer. "What gives?"

"Your leg. What happened to that machine thing you had?"

Kenneth let out a nervous laugh. "Oh, that . . . It came back. I could show you the—"

The glasses I wore blazed with a red-orange flare. It rippled around the man, shredding the glamour around him. It wasn't Kenneth. Beneath the glamour was the undead face of Clarence Goins, the corpse I had tried to save yesterday. "Clarence?"

"Damn glasses," he snapped. Slapping my gun to the side, he bulled forward with a fist, socking me in the jaw.

Dazed from the punch, I tried to pull back. Clarence didn't give me a chance. Lashing out with a foot, he kicked the gun away.

"What the shit, Clarence?" I asked. He looked at me with undead eyes, and for a moment, I was confused. "Are you a Dead Man, now?"

"Something like that." He streaked toward me and caught me in the ribs with a right hook. It hurt. Felt like a concrete pylon had just hit me in the side. My protection from the Powers That Be was good, but it was iffy if it went up against itself.

Recovering, I backpedaled, my back hitting one of the large warehouse's big support beams.

"What's going on, Clarence?"

"Let's just say, you have more than a few enemies who are willing to put a Dead Man contract on you."

Who? I wondered, though I knew that was a list longer than my arm. Even before I was a Dead Man, I'd had enemies on Earth. Had they tracked me here after Hell? I struggled to figure out what to do, my body still recovering from the bullets that had torn away bits of my soul.

"Knew you would overdo it, Gallic," Clarence said, though his voice was different. Something familiar in it made me wince.

"Say my name again."

There was a slight smirk on the undead man's face. "You figure it out, Gallic? Recognize me?"

The person wearing the Clarence face took a step back, lips twisting in a smirk.

"Yeah, I recognize you. What do you want, Turning?"

The form of Clarence let out a laugh. "Knew you'd figure it out." He reached up and peeled off Clarence's face, revealing the horribly scarred face beneath. It was William Turning, Nightside resident, criminal, and thorn in my side for far, far too long. His smile was more disturbing, like a rictus of a painful smirk.

"Nightside needs your services, John Gallic."

Enter Typhon

I narrowed my eyes at William. "Why the fuck should I follow you?"

"As I said, Nightside needs you." He turned and started to walk away slowly, his left leg dragging a little before he could move it, and always a slight drop when he put weight on his left. I gave him that limp. But that's a story for another time.

"I need to solve Kenneth's case first."

"All part of the same case," he said, moving closer to the back wall of the storeroom. The lights in that part of the large storage area weren't as bright. But I could almost feel a breach in the Barrier there. With my connection to Janus City proper, I knew where the divider was at all times. And the Barrier was on the other side of the storeroom wall.

"Who's on the other side?" I asked, not moving yet.

"Typhon."

"Fuck, why him?"

"He won't work with anyone else."

I hated having to deal with Nightsider. Especially Typhon. But it happens now and then. Nightside is, well, it's a pit. Dayside isn't a crown jewel either, but it's better than a perpetually dark trash heap of an alternate dimension. And of course, I had to deal with Typhon—the weird, creepy bastard who was a Dead Man and not a Dead Man.

I moved toward William who had placed a hand on the wall and was chanting some incantation or another. I didn't know what he said; the words went in one ear and out the other. As a Dead Man, I had some inherent magic at my disposal, yet I couldn't learn anything new. The Powers That Be enjoyed that, the pricks.

There was a sudden blast of dank, fetid air from the darkness that crept along the wall of the storehouse. That was the stench of Nightside. William gestured toward the darkness, and I saw a humanoid shape resolve itself in the center. It was a distorted human shape, yet there were two glowing yellow eyes.

Typhon.

Glaring at me from behind glasses like mine, and yet not. They were a part of his face. No one knew what his actual face looked like; it was covered by a mask. His eyes, though, they pierced my soul.

"Fucking creep," I said, moving closer to the dark tunnel. "You have an extra payment?"

"I'm not creepy, you are," Typhon hissed in my head.

And then there's the fact that he can read my mind and speak in my head. *No, not creepy at all, ugly.*

"Look who's talking," Typhon responded in my head.

I gave him a grin. "Been awhile, Ty. How they hanging?"

"Low and to the left."

I raised an eyebrow. "Got my stuff?"

"Would I be here if I didn't, John?" Typhon's thin mask pulled taunt in a grin while holding a bottle. "But I need you to come through."

"Could be here just to fuck with me," I said. "What's the play?"

He gave me look. "Sounds like something I'd do," he whispered in my head. "Promise, just a bit of help with my case and I'll help you with yours."

"You're an asshole."

"Takes one to know one."

"Show me."

He nodded and held up a small bottle of Johnnie Walker Black. I slammed back the scotch, letting the burn trickle down my throat and belly. I stepped through the portal. I passed through the strange greasy film that was the center of the Barrier, the exact moment I passed into Nightside. A chill hit me as I stepped into Typhon's office.

It was the usual thing, a few beaten up dark leather chairs, patched and repatched enough that the upholstery looked more like a quilt. There was a desk that had seen better days, a file cabinet, and a window that looked out onto the back alley behind his office, though the glass was frosted.

A bright red neon sign outside caused the frosted glass to glow a malevolent reddish hue, bathing the office in a patina of blood.

Typhon waited a few moments as I took another long gulp and settled into a chair, then leaned forward, hands held out. I held up a hand to stop him and took one last deep swallow before handing the bottle back to him.

"Fuck I needed that." I sighed, smacking my lips.

"Why are you here, John?"

"I was told I was going to be working with you," I said, looking between him and William. William gave me a slight grin, as if he was the smartest one in the room.

Typhon snapped his head toward the smiling William. "What the fuck is wrong with you?"

Typhon was screaming in William's head loud enough that there was leakage. Even *my* skull throbbed. I couldn't imagine what William was experiencing. I looked him over, and the Dead Man looked like he was about to pass out.

"You said get the best," William said in a halting voice.

I turned to look at Typhon. "I'm touched, Ty."

"Fuck you, Gallic," Typhon snapped in my head. "You're the best on such short notice." Typhon looked at William. "You, I'll deal with later. Get out."

William held his hands up, gave a slight shrug and then turned and did his dragging limp walk out of the office.

"Still taking it as a compliment," I said, more to myself than Tyhon once William left. I did reach out and snag the bottle of Johnnie Black and took another belt. "Why am I here?"

"You need to know what I'm up to for that," Typhon said. He walked toward me, and I wanted to bolt.

"Not a—"

"Yes, you gotta get up to speed in a hurry. Mind-link is the quick and dirty way."

"Fuck you," I said as his palm connected with my forehead and a sudden rush of memories came to me in one painful thrust.

Who is Roxanne List?

Typhon leered at the woman grinding around on the pole. He peeled off another double sawbuck from the roll in his jacket and slid it toward her. The catgirl gave him a happy squeak and crawled toward him, her yellow cat eyes staring at him as she did. She leaned forward, arching her back as she did to show off her ass in the too-small thong that blended well with her soft yellow-furred body. She opened her mouth, took the bill between her teeth, and jerked backwards to sit up, revealing her fur-sheathed body. Her small pert breasts were revealed as the yellow fur faded to a thin fuzz that disappeared a scant inch from her areolae.

"Always my favorite," he said to her in her head.

She gave him a confused look.

He shook his head and started to get up. She crawled forward again and gave him a mewling whimper. He peeled off two more bills, pressed them to the glowing dance floor, and slid them toward her. She gave him a large smile, mostly human with only the incisors being more cat-like.

Again, she gave him a squeak and happy meow.

He gave a look at the bouncer, Xer, on his way to the door. The thick-shouldered brute grunted at Typhon as he walked past, but settled a thick meaty hand on Typhon's shoulder. "Don't you usually leave after her set?"

"Need to get back to the wife," Typhon whispered. Xer's face twisted strangely at hearing Typhon's voice in his head. Xer let him go, and Typhon took the opportunity to leave the strip club.

Outside, the perpetual umber of Janus City's Eastside was lit with the neon signs of the red-light district and a few actual red lanterns hanging outside of several apartments and homes. Typhon walked along the street, unable to contain the thoughts that streamed into his mind. In the club, it had been easy to wall off his thoughts from everyone else. Attention was elsewhere and focused on the girls. Out in the city, it was harder to push away the stray thoughts that assaulted him as he walked down the street. He wanted to get home, and soon.

Home. His sanctuary, the one place where he could find peace and was able to sleep. Thick plates of silver and gold were mounted on the walls of the small apartment. It had cost him a pretty penny, yet it was worth it to have a place to rest his head and escape the constant barrage of others' thoughts, dreams, and nightmares.

But then, Typhon also needed those thoughts at times. It was his stock and trade.

Other people's secrets.

As his steps found the *Wraith Hostel,* he stopped short. One sentence slammed into his head.

"I will kill them all."

Typhon closed his eyes and tried to focus on the thought. He felt a strong surge of hate for a long moment and searched for the source. Rain started to fall, steady, hard rain that he hated since it distorted his power, his gift.

The surge of hate vanished.

Dammit. He was stuck. Part of him wanted to wait again for the angry thought. Someone wanted to kill people. It wasn't an unfamiliar sentiment. Typhon himself wished he could kill the city at times. Yet, there hadn't been a spike of sudden anger in this thought. It was a deep hatred for the world at large, from someone—or something—that wanted to act on that hatred.

It was also something he could usually track, yet the rain hindered his ability. And it would only get worse. Defeated for the moment, he went inside. Opening the door, he was knocked to the side by a teenage girl as she rushed past him. She was thick, blue and pink hair flaring around her as she rushed past. She gave him a dirty look and walked off into the rain.

Typhon shook his head and walked into the *Wraith Hostel.* He checked his mail, gave a nod to his neighbor Mrs. Gertz. She had been dead for five years but wasn't a rez job. She was a ghost who still believed she was alive. That happened often in Eastside.

He kept going up the stairs, three flights to his small room. The door had been broken open. He frowned and concentrated, but nobody was inside. He opened his door and found his small place had been ransacked. His stomach knotted and for a second, he reached out with his mind to touch the secret compartment in the bedroom. *Still safe.* A small bit of relief washed over him. It was dark as he entered, when Typhon righted the lamp and switched it on, he was shocked to find a man sitting his chair, a smile on his round fleshy face.

"Hello, Typhon. I can see you're surprised I was to find your place."

Typhon glared at the man.

"Yes, I also know about your small issue with not being able to talk," the man said. "My name is Grenden. And before you stress yourself more, this is the reason you can't hear my thoughts." Grenden took a thick meaty hand and pulled a small pendant out from under his shirt. The gray-suited man smirked when Typhon's eyes fell upon it.

"Yes, it's a mind shield. Not an inexpensive item." He let out a small laugh. "Now, please have a seat on that wretched thing you call a couch."

Typhon smirked at the man. He liked the couch. It was a paisley thing that was overstuffed and extremely comfortable. He flopped down on it, then looked at Grenden.

"I need you to find someone for me. Her name is Roxanne List."

Grenden's Deal

I shoved away from Typhon. "So, you need help finding her?"

Without a word, he was on top of me again. I was so close; the thin material of his mask revealed a smirk as Typhon clamped both hands on my temples. I was rocked backwards into his mind again.

Typhon had heard the name somewhere before but couldn't place it. "Who's that?"

Grendel chuckled. "I feel a little tremble on my chest. So, you must be trying to talk to me. Ha-ha. Not going to help. I assume you're asking who that is. She's a woman who stole something from my penthouse at the *Westron*. Something I very much wish to get back."

Typhon narrowed his eyes. *Swanky place*, he thought. He hated what he was about to do. He worked saliva into his mouth, feeling the scars on the interior. He took breath and asked in a very pained and rasping voice, "What did she steal?"

"Ahh, so you *can* speak. I had heard it was bit of a mystery if you could or not."

"Not something I like to do." He let out a low growl, his throat hurting from such long disuse.

"I see. To your question, she stole a piece of artwork. Nothing to concern yourself with. I simply want her found and held for my own, hee-hee, punishment."

"Payment?"

Grenden smirked. "Ten thousand."

Typhoon walked closer to the large fleshy man and stuck out his hand. Ten thousand was enough to sustain him for some time. He might even afford a ticket to Westside for a few days, spend some time at Eden Falls. "Deal."

Grenden wrapped his fat hand around Typhon's slender one and jolted from the contact. "What was that?"

"You made a deal, a contract," Typhon said, moving his neck back and forth, his voice stronger. He stood straighter and renewed energy flooded his body.

Grenden collapsed back into the chair, weak as a kitten. "What . . . What did you—" He gasped, unable to speak completely.

Typhon smirked. He ran his tongue along the inside of his mouth and felt the scars fading. "You made a deal in Nightside, Mr. Grenden. You said you knew what I am. You don't. I'll find this woman for you. But you aren't going anywhere. You won't be able to move until I return with your target."

"What—"

"I've taken your energy, a piece of your soul. You're going to help me with this case, and I'll know exactly where you are while I'm out and about." He let out a sigh and stretched out his back and cracked his neck, moving it back and forth a few times, then turned to walk away.

"You mean I'm stuck here?"

"Most assuredly," Typhon said as he walked out the door.

Outside, the rain had slackened yet hadn't stopped. It was enough to cause annoyance. After the infusion from Grenden, Typhon felt better than he had in some time. It had been a while since he'd had a case. He hadn't taken many since the accident.

His tongue sought the scars again. They had faded to almost nothing, but he still felt a small runnel of flesh as his tongue touched his upper palate.

He had no idea who Roxanne List was, but Grenden did. And she had stolen something from him. Where to start? The last place Grenden knew where she was—the Westron Penthouse here the artwork was stolen. It was as good a place as any to head to and search for clues.

"So, that is where I come in?" I asked, looking up at Typhon as he pulled away.

"Yup," Typhon said with a rasping voice.

"How long is your contract?"

"Two weeks, give or take," Typhon said with a shrug.

I didn't want to question him. I saw what his contract had done to Grenden. I wondered if two weeks was how long Grenden had to survive, but I didn't want to ask that.

"To the *Westron*?" I asked. When Typhon gave me a head bob, I gestured towards the door. "Lead the way, creepy."

Don't miss out!

Visit the website below and you can sign up to receive emails whenever Lon E. Varnadore publishes a new book. There's no charge and no obligation.

https://books2read.com/r/B-A-MEQJ-JBXVB

Connecting independent readers to independent writers.